THE LITTLE KNIGHT'S DRAGON

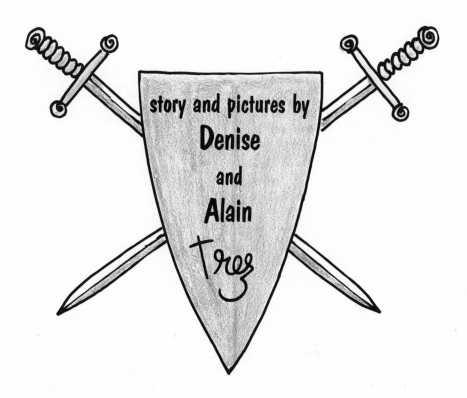

story and pictures by
Denise
and
Alain
Trez

THE WORLD PUBLISHING COMPANY · CLEVELAND AND NEW YORK

Published by The World Publishing Company, 2231 West 110th Street, Cleveland 2, Ohio

Published simultaneously in Canada by Nelson, Foster & Scott Ltd.

Library of Congress Catalog Card Number: 63-8910

4 5 67

THE LITTLE KNIGHT'S DRAGON

Once upon a time in a very large castle there lived a small boy whose father was a great knight.

The little boy preferred playing marbles,

but every night he listened to stories about his father's famous deeds....

And every day he looked at the paintings

in the Great Gallery that portrayed them.

At the very end of the gallery
was a space without a painting. When the little boy asked why,
his nurse explained that it was being saved for the next exploit of his father's.

There was in the country a dragon so terrible that no one dared kill it. This dragon had kidnapped a little princess.

"He will eat her when she is fifteen years old," said the little boy's nurse. "But your father is very brave and he will rescue her before then. Every day he practices to fight the dragon."

The little boy was proud of his father's courage, but he felt sorry for the little girl. It would be sad to be the prisoner of a dragon, and he thought she must

be afraid to be all alone in a tower. So one night he got out of bed very quietly and mounted his horse.

He had decided to go to the rescue of the princess himself, but he didn't know exactly which direction to take. Just then, a mouse frightened the horse and

away it galloped. It ran and ran until it came to a huge tree in the path. The horse braked with his front feet . . . and the little boy was tossed headfirst. . . .

The tree swayed and crashed over a log. Wham! The dragon, who lived
near-by, ran out of his castle and put his heavy foot on the branches to

see better what was happening. The trunk tilted up and, again, the
little knight soared into the air. . . .

The little princess, who was watching from
the tower window, reached out to catch him.

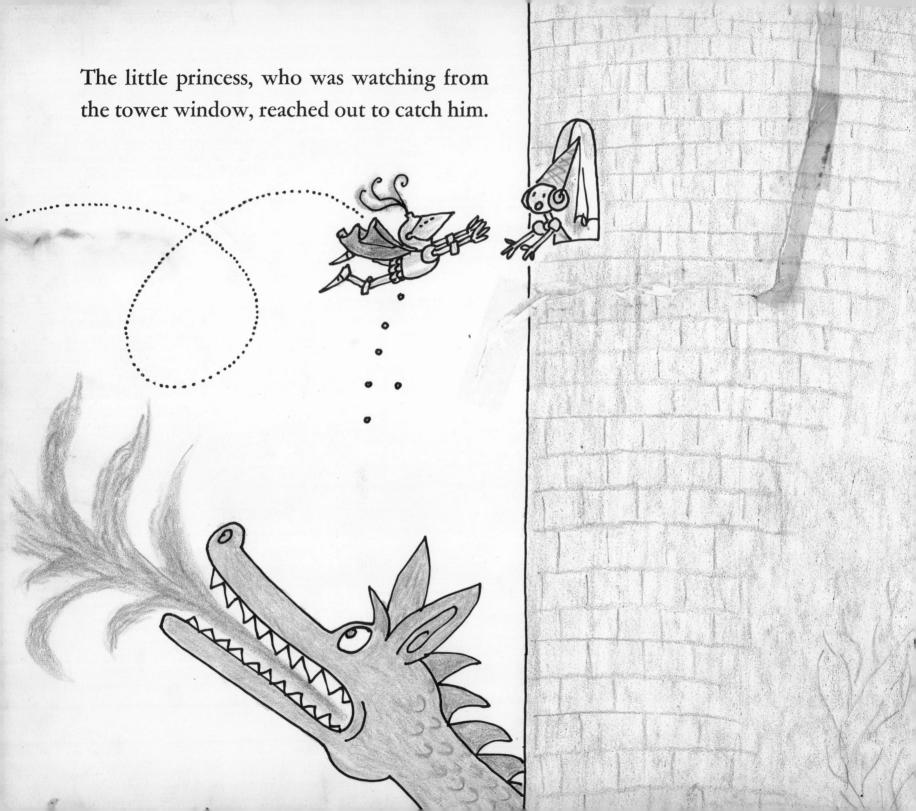

She leaned too far and
they fell together.
Fortunately, the princess'
skirt ballooned into a
parachute for them.

But the dragon was no longer interested; he was curious about the marbles that had fallen from the little knight's pocket. What were they for?

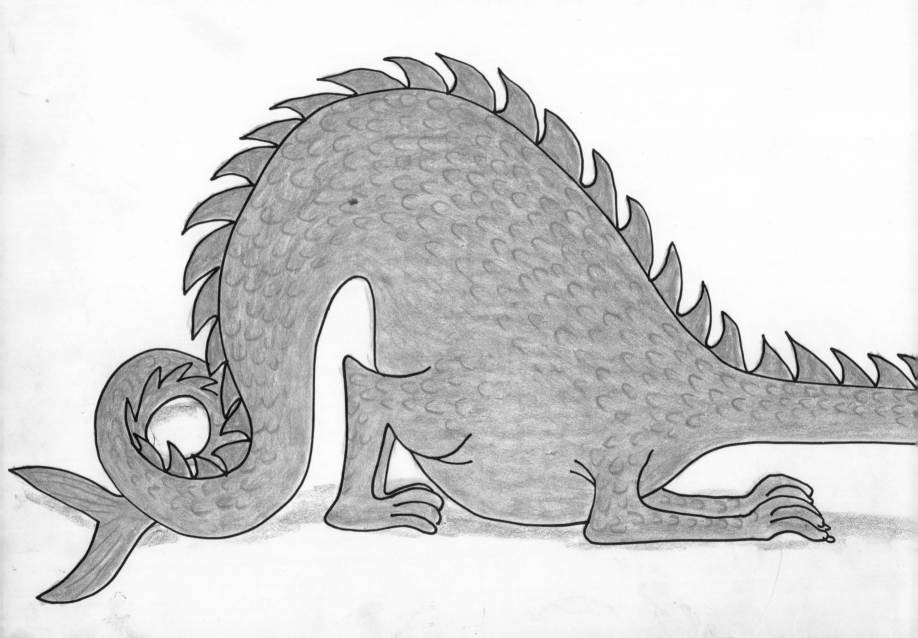

Forgetting completely that dragons are dangerous, the little knight showed him how to play the game. The dragon was enchanted.

When it was time to return to the little

knight's castle, the dragon followed them.

You can imagine the hub-
bub when the guards
sighted the dragon! The
little knight's father galloped forward to kill the
monster.

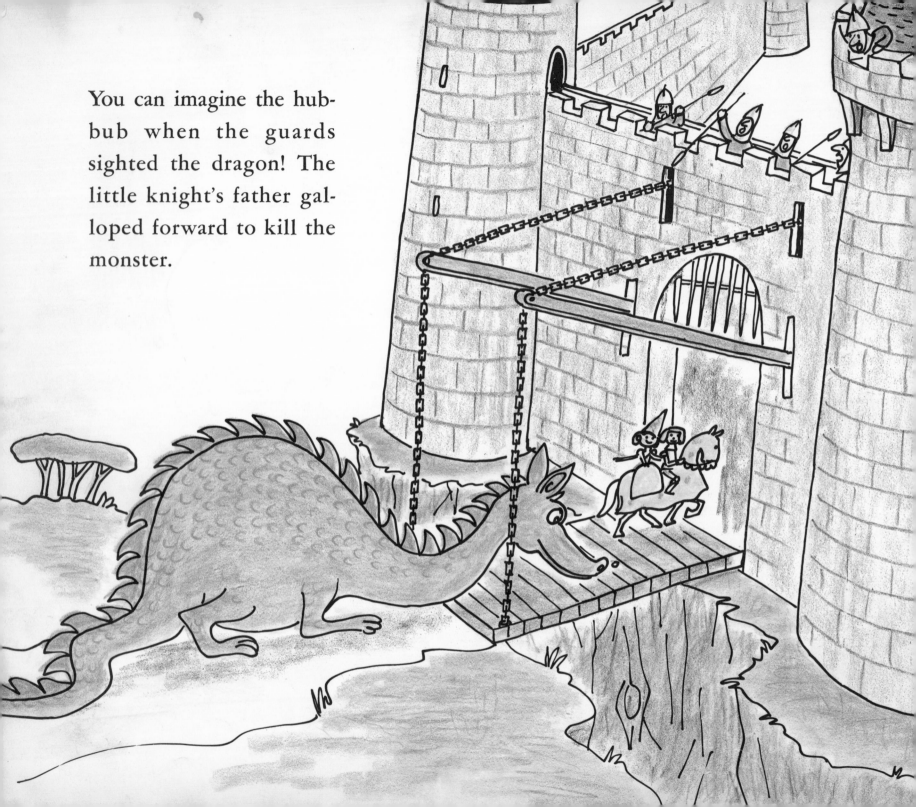

But the children assured him there was no danger; the dragon would be very useful. They put him in the great courtyard where he spent the summer playing marbles.

In the winter he stayed in the cellar and provided central heating for the whole castle.

Everyone was happy. They painted a fine picture in honor of the little knight in the empty space at the end of the Great Gallery. When he grew up he married the princess, and they had many children...

and many, many little dragons.